Inspired by Monica Reid and her
pet tortoise, Speedy.

Monica Pink
Pet Shrink

Written by Frances O'Neill
Illustrated by Xiaoyi Hu

SAINTED
MEDIA

Table of Contents

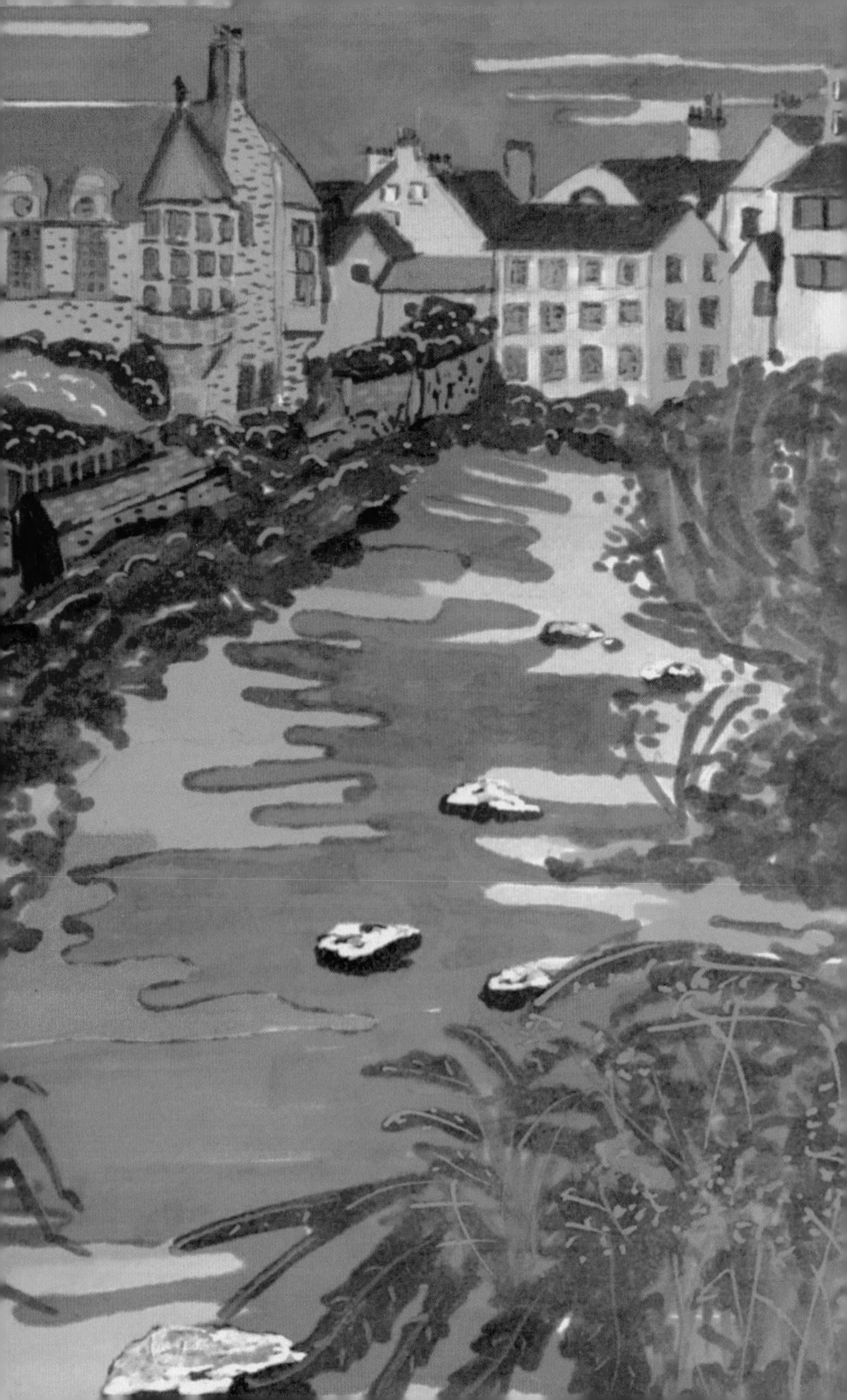

My name is Monica Pink and this is the story of how I became a Pet Shrink.

A Pet Shrink is someone who is really good at understanding pets. I am very good at understanding pets, but sometimes I am not very good at understanding people - especially grown-ups!

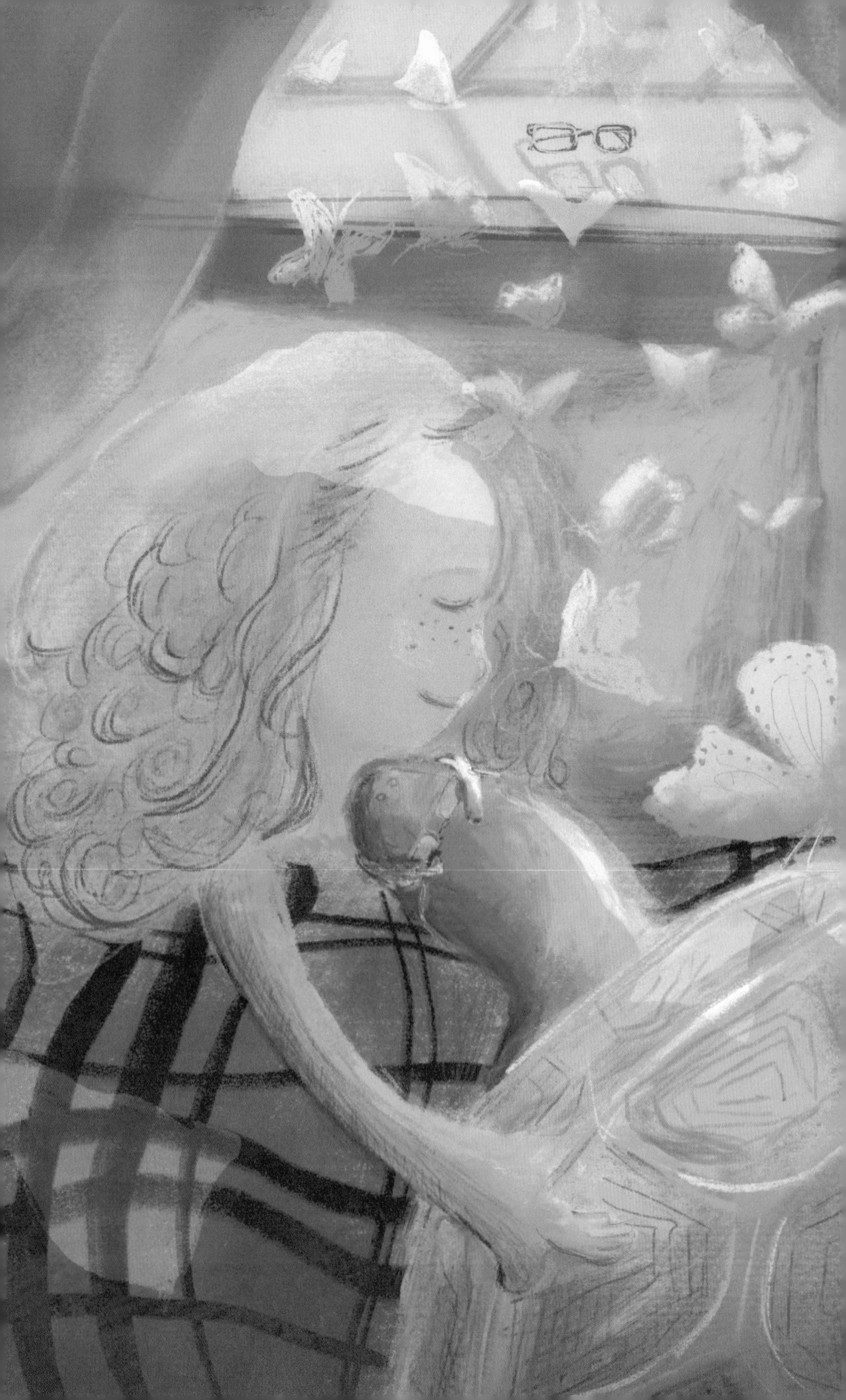

Chapter 1

May Day

I woke up with Speedy sniffing my neck. Speedy is the cleverest tortoise on the planet, he is 70 years old and my dad said he used to belong to my granddad. I never knew my granddad, my dad never talks about him so I think my granddad's probably dead.

It's May Day today, which I think means that everyone gets a day off. I wonder what kids with brothers and sisters talk about on May Day. I only get to talk to Speedy and he usually doesn't talk back - I usually know what he is thinking though.

I asked him what he dreamed about and I knew that the answer was butterflies because that's what I was dreaming about too. Me and Speedy always dream about the same stuff - we have a connection.

Dad always puts the roaring lion alarm clock in the living room so that mum has to get up to switch it off. I don't think mum likes lions very much - this morning she hit the lion alarm clock with her pink fluffy slippers.

'Your mother isn't a morning person

Monica, she's not a lark like you and me.'

Mum just growled at my dad like a snarly dog. I think mum is an owl but I can't be sure, as I've never heard her say, 'I'm up with the owls.' I think owls are a bit strange with their big eyes and their twisty necks, no wonder they hide in the dark. If I looked like an owl, I'd hide in the dark too.

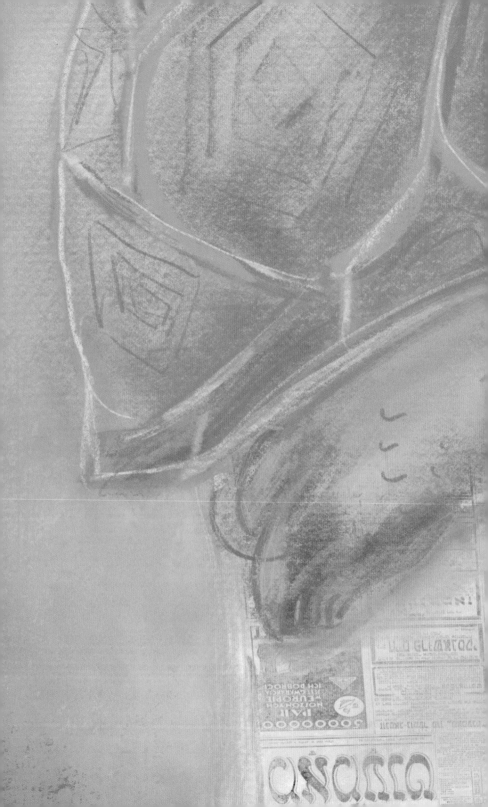

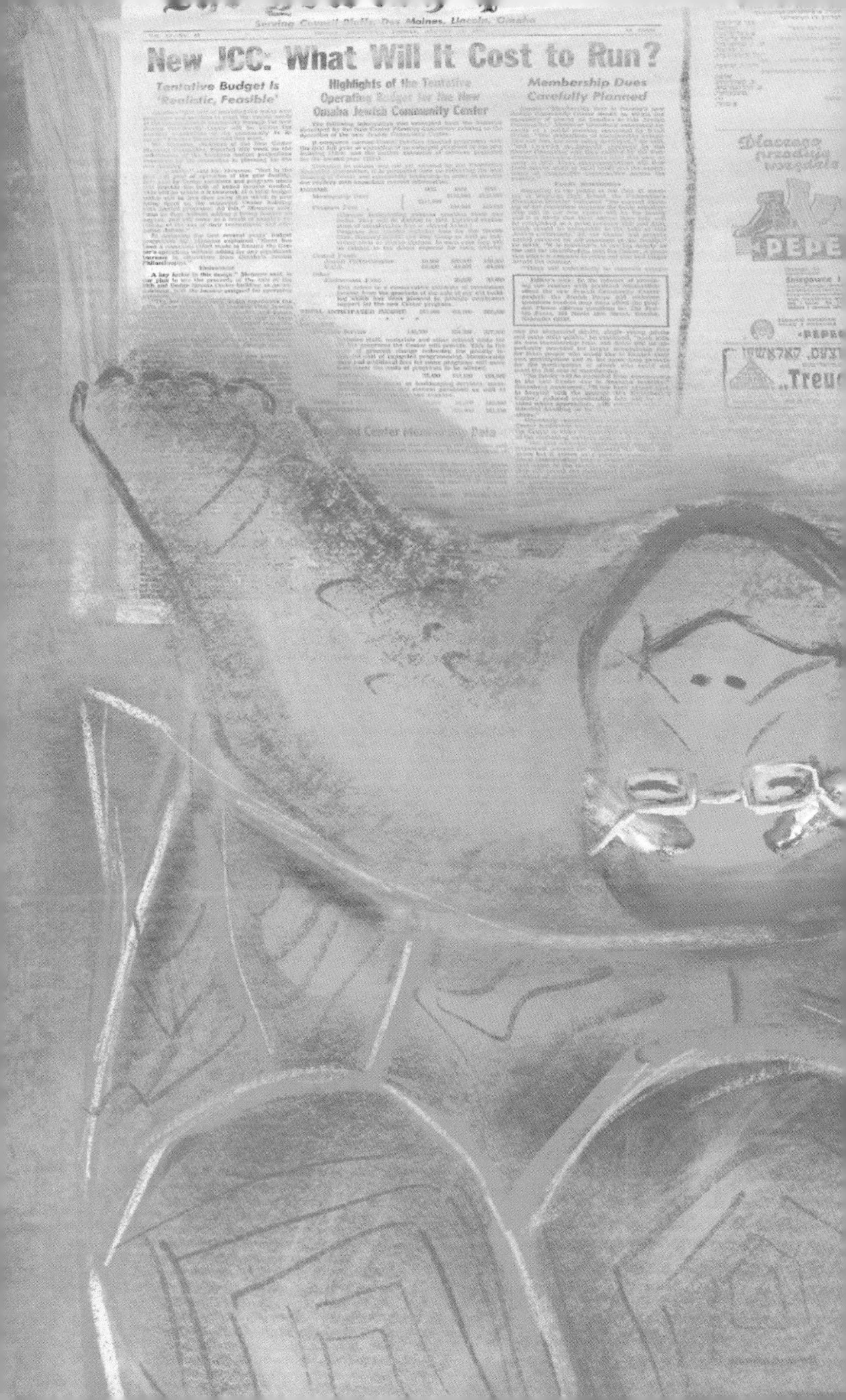

Serving Council Bluffs, Des Moines, Lincoln, Omaha
New JCC: What Will It Cost to Run?
Tentative Budget Is 'Realistic, Feasible'
Highlights of the Tentative Operating Budget for the New Omaha Jewish Community Center
Membership Dues Carefully Planned

Chapter 2

Speedy Speedy

As it was a holiday, dad said Speedy was allowed an extra leaf, mum was allowed an extra 5 grams of butter and I was allowed half a bowl of Coco Pops. I love Coco Pops, the pops are much tastier than porridge.

I wonder if Speedy would like Coco Pops - he is always really slow at doing everything, maybe some fast energy would be a nice change for him. I was so full of fast Coco Pop energy I asked dad if I could take Speedy for a walk to the shops. Dad said, 'Just so long as you keep him on a lead.' Mum said, 'Are you worried he might run away to the circus, Ken?'

Dad looked annoyed, he put his newspaper up and hid behind it. I asked mum why Speedy would run away and she said because of malnutrition. I asked mum if she wanted anything from the shops and she whispered, 'Chocolate.'

And then dad said from behind his newspaper, 'Remember your figure Barb, I didn't marry the local Beauty Queen to see her turn into the Village Chubber.'

Mum stuck her tongue out and then it looked like she mouthed, 'I hate your guts.' It seems that dad can see through newspapers, he pushed his chair out, all angry and annoyed and just as he stomped towards the back door, he slipped on Speedy's poo. He grabbed Speedy and slammed the door shut behind them.

I ran to the other room and looked out of the window so that I could see where dad had put Speedy. I heard the roaring sound of dad's big red tractor lawn mower. He always cuts the grass really fast when he is angry. I could see dad swishing by the window but I couldn't see Speedy. I opened the window and shouted, 'Are you OK Speedy, it the noise too loud for you?'

And then I saw Speedy fly through the sky, I heard a big crash and what sounded like an Easter egg hitting a tree.

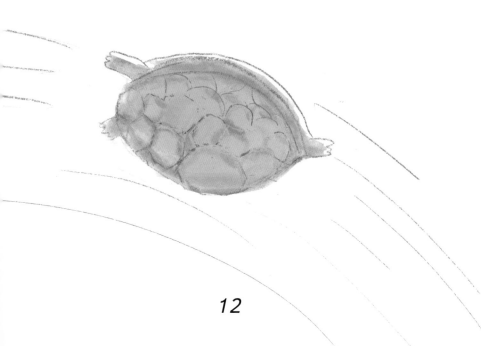

Chapter 3

The Funeral

Dad had tried to miss Speedy and crashed into the tree. 'They were both killed instantly,' is what the doctor said. I think he wants us to be happy that they were both killed instantly but I'm not sure why.

Me and mum were in a big black car, dad was in a long car in a coffin. Mum couldn't get the gates to open, they got stuck half way and the cars had to squeeze out. Mum threw the remote control for the gates out of the car window.

A big messy van appeared from nowhere, it screeched around the corner with its squeaky brakes and scraped all the way along dad's car and then it scraped all the way along our car. Mum's mouth fell open but she didn't scream or say anything. The rusty old van said **Joe Strange Animal Sanctuary** on it. At the back of the van a boy with really messy hair and freckles looked out. He held up an armadillo to the window and waved the little armadillo's paw at me. I couldn't help but smile.

Me and mum both wore matching black outfits, we stood by the side of the grave as they lowered dad's coffin in.

Miss Appleby was very nice and asked mum when I would be coming back to school. Mum didn't answer and looked a little confused. Eventually mum said, 'Ken made all the decisions in the house.'

Now it was Miss Appleby's turn to be confused. Dr Dickson was also there and he made a beeline for mum. Bees make beelines for honey by doing a wiggily-waggle dance. Bees have very small brains. I think Dr Dickson has a lot in common with bees. I'd like him to dance into a giant pot of honey and get stuck there forever.

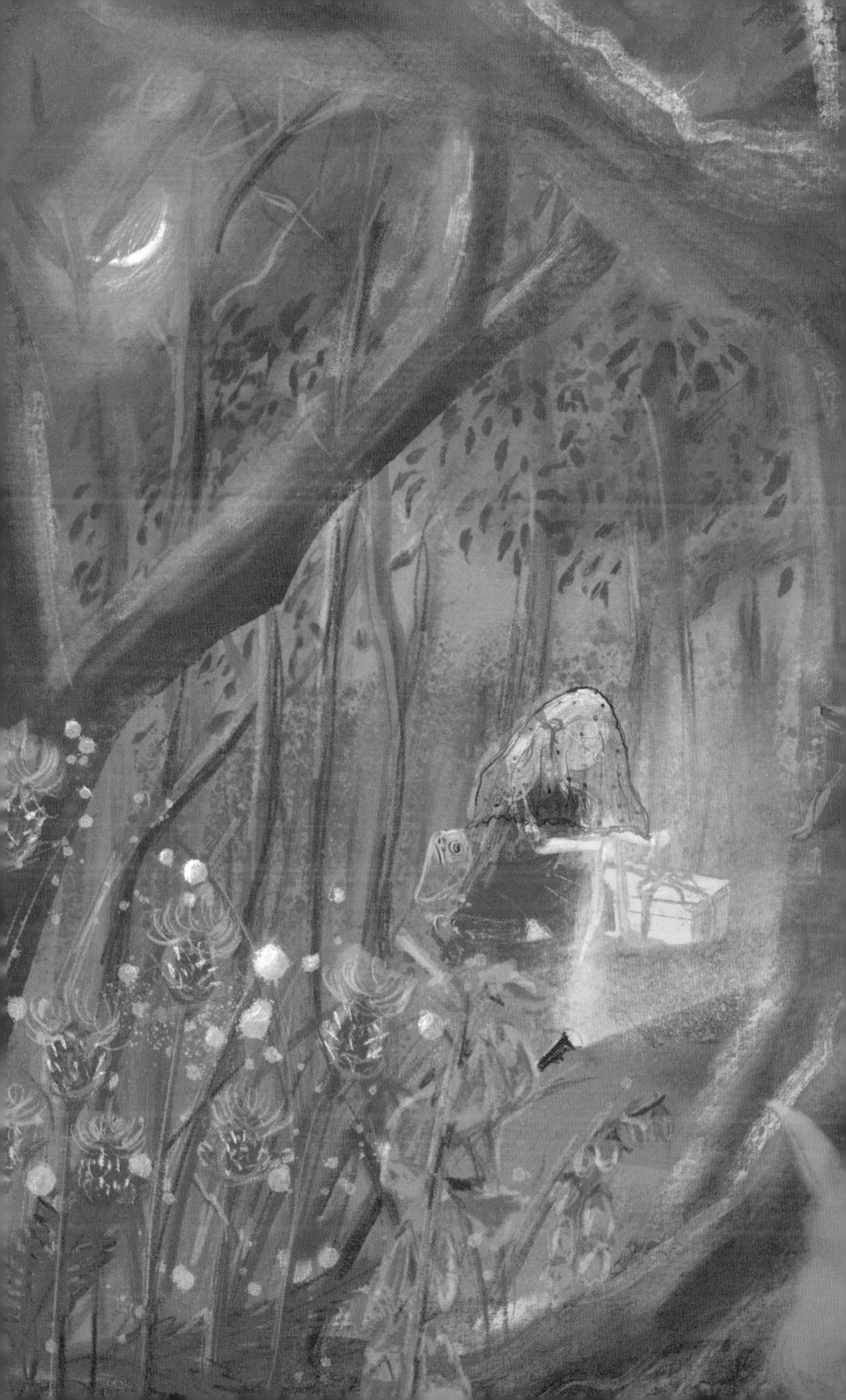

I just want dad to come back and set the roaring lion alarm clock and then in the morning everything will be just fine again.

This evening I decided it was time I buried Speedy. Mum said she didn't want to have a dead tortoise in the glass case in the kitchen any longer. I went out with a very nice black net curtain veil over my black dress and dug a grave for Speedy at the bottom of the garden. It was dark so I had to use a torch. I put Speedy in a shoebox with red ribbons around the box. I lowered Speedy's shoebox coffin into the grave as slowly as I could.

I took a picture of Speedy's grave - I wish he could see it. I think he'd like it.

The lion alarm clock rang but mum wouldn't get up and when I tried to tell her what time it was, she pulled the covers over her head. I asked her if I could go to school and she didn't answer. I sat at the kitchen table in my black PJs and waited for mum to come in and make me breakfast.

I think I'll wear black forever. Mum didn't get up for breakfast and so I poured myself a full bowl of Coco Pops and I didn't even eat all of them. I wish dad was here to make me some slow energy porridge. I stared at Speedy's empty glass case for a long time.

I decided it was time I put Speedy's things in the bin. Looking at his empty glass case and his old toys just made me sad. I carried his case to the outside bin. I tipped as much as I could into the bin and then I noticed Dr Dickson standing next to me. He had snuck up on me like a sneaky snake.

He looked inside the bin and said, **'Surprisingly smelly little critters,'** and then he sneezed and sneezed and sneezed.

Oh don't say sorry Dr Dickson, just

sneeze your slimey green snot all over me, I thought.

Dr Dickson said he wanted to know when I was coming back to school, that all my classmates missed me. Well I knew that was a lie right away. Then he asked if he could speak to mum and I told him that she was sleeping.

My dad says, 'The thing about lying is that it's infectious and so you should never start.' Well Dr Dickson is like an infectious disease and he started it and he should know better cause he's a grown up and I'm just a kid. Mum took out all the photos she could find and looked through them, every time she came to a picture of dad her eyes filled with tears. I found a picture of Speedy, my eyes also filled with tears.

The thing about tears is that they're infectious and you'd better not start crying or everyone will start crying too. I just made that up but I think it could be true. I blinked away my tears because I have to be strong for mum.

The doorbell rang and I answered and it was Dr Sneaky Snake Dickson. **'My mum's still sleeping,'** I said and closed the door in his face.

I wish Speedy was here and I wish I could talk to him. I didn't really know how much I loved Speedy, it is hard to explain how much I miss him. I wish more than anything that dad hadn't killed him.

Before I went to bed I tried to contact Speedy by sitting at the kitchen table with the lights off and a candle on. I put my black net curtain veil over my head and I had a picture of Speedy and I said over and over, '**Talk to me Speedy.**'

But nothing happened and then mum put the light on. She looked confused.

I asked mum if dad would go to heaven even though he had killed Speedy. Mum didn't answer my question and sent me to bed. The phone rang and it was Dr Dickson - I should have unplugged the phone and now it is too late. I heard mum arranging to meet him.

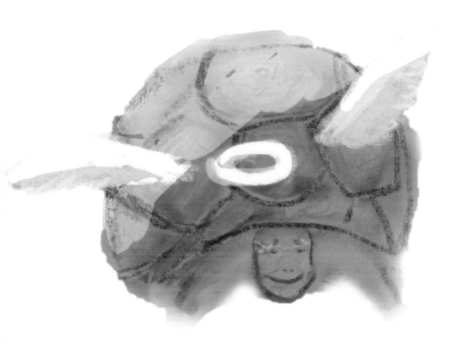

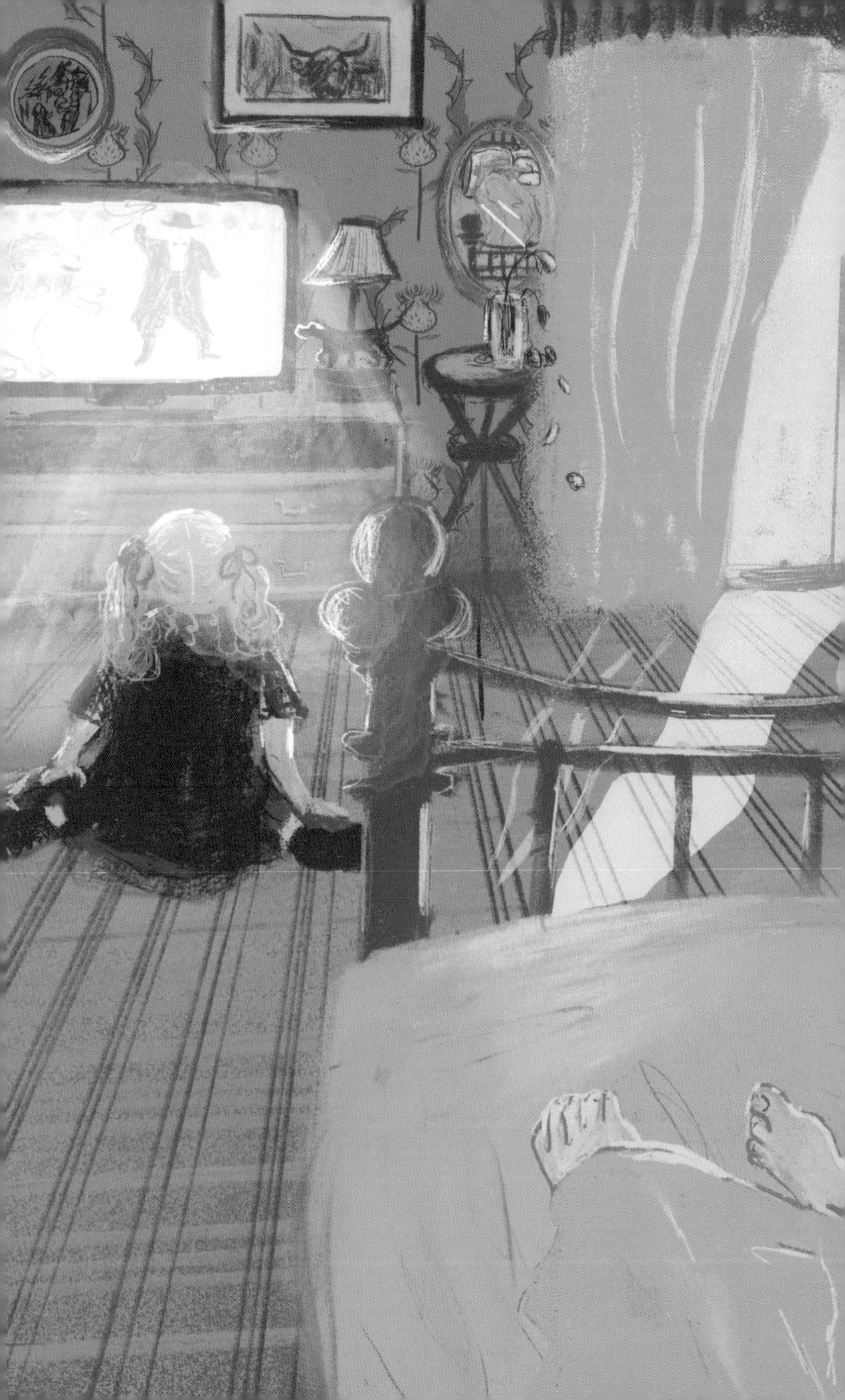

Chapter 4

Fearless Fred

The most amazing thing ever happened today. I was watching TV in mum's room, she was in bed with her head under the covers and the TV was on - so I sat on the floor and stared at the TV and I saw dad.

He was pretending to be Fearless Fred, a lion tamer. He was dressed in a funny lion-taming outfit, he looked a bit like Indiana Jones and he stared straight out of the TV and said in a funny voice, 'The only way to soften a lion's heart is to look straight into its eyes and send it a message of love.' And dad looked straight into my eyes and I felt a message of love go between us and then I said, 'It's okay dad, your secret is safe with me.'

I now know that dad pretended to be dead and then ran away to the circus because he felt so bad about killing Speedy. 'I forgive you dad and I love you - I wish you would come home soon.'

I asked mum if I could have a new pet and she said she would have to think about it. I wish I had a lion for a pet.

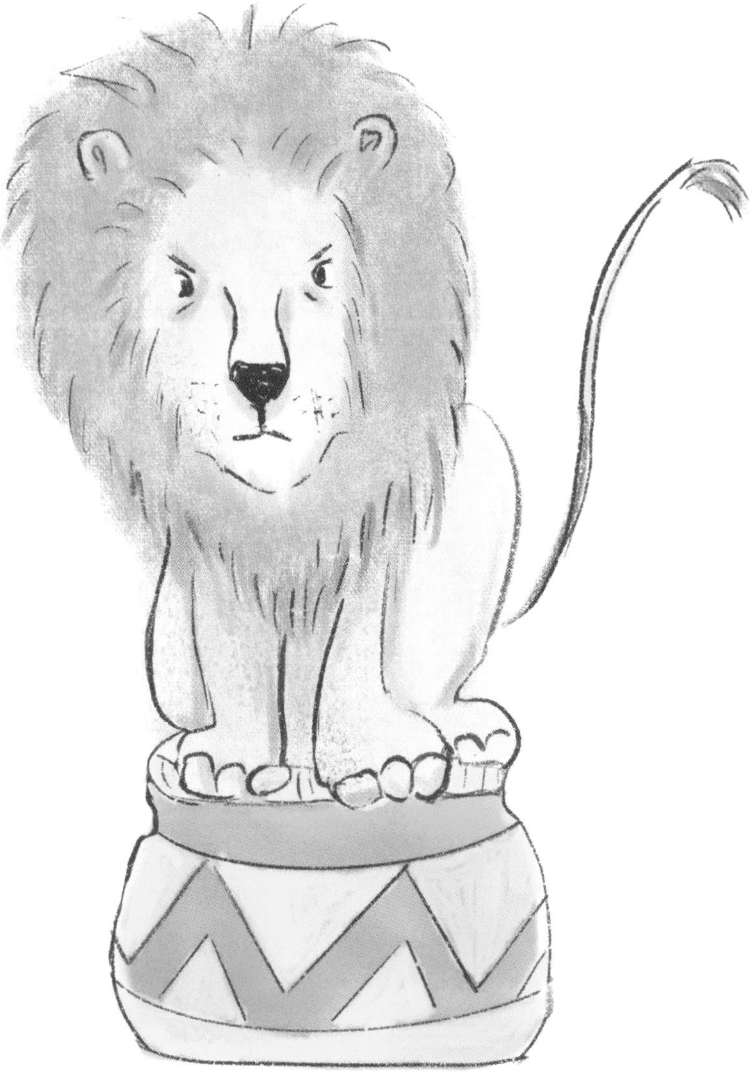

Chapter 5

The Crazy Haired Neighbours

Today I was in the attic. Mum had put dad's clothes up there and I had to go and bring them down as I knew dad would be back one day and would want to wear them. I heard the noise of a big truck and so I climbed up on an old chest and looked out of the window. And what I saw was amazing.

I saw two big trucks outside the gigantic house next door and the boy with the crazy hair from the funeral day and his crazy haired dad jumping up and down with excitedness. They opened the back of one of the trucks and inside were lots and lots of animals and pets. The boy let some geese out and they ran around the garden. The boy knew I was watching him and he looked up at me, I jumped down.

I studied the chest I had been standing on - it was like a Pirate's chest and it had a padlock on it. I opened the padlock with the end of a ladybird clasp from my hair. I opened the chest and inside it I found a lion tamer's whip and a poster of Fearless

Fred. The poster was written in a funny language. I kissed the poster.

Chapter 6

Back To School

When I went to school today all the kids danced round me and sang, 'Your dad's dead, your dad's dead, you ain't got a dad. Monica Pink's dad's dead.'

But they don't know that my dad is really a lion tamer and if they did know they wouldn't be singing their stupid little song.

I thought of Fearless Fred and I made the sound of a lion roaring - the kids laughed at me.

Mark Dickson started the singing again and the other kids joined in because they always do what he says. Dr Dickson came across the playground and hit Mark Dickson across the head. I don't think it was very nice of him to hit him, even if he is his uncle and even if Mark Dickson is really annoying.

The messy haired, freckly boy, from next door sat next to me in class. He is called William Strange and he knows lots and lots of stuff about pets. I like him. He is the first kid I have ever met who knows more than me about pets.

Stuff William knows about Henry the class Hamster and other hamsters.

1. Hamsters usually live until they are 3.
2. Hamsters don't like to share their homes with other hamsters.
3. Hamster is a German word for keeping food in your cheeks.

I asked William why hamsters don't like to share their homes and he didn't know.

I think that hamsters are probably a little bit selfish because selfish people don't like to share and that would explain why they hide all their food in their cheeks

- not people but hamsters. But I guess that selfish kids might keep all their sweeties in their cheeks.

Miss Appleby called me to the front of the class and she told me to go to Dr Dickson's office. She said, 'The world feels like a better place when you smile and you have such a beautiful smile, Monica Pink.'

I tried my best to smile because I like Miss Appleby very much but inside I felt scared because I didn't want to go and see Dr Dickson.

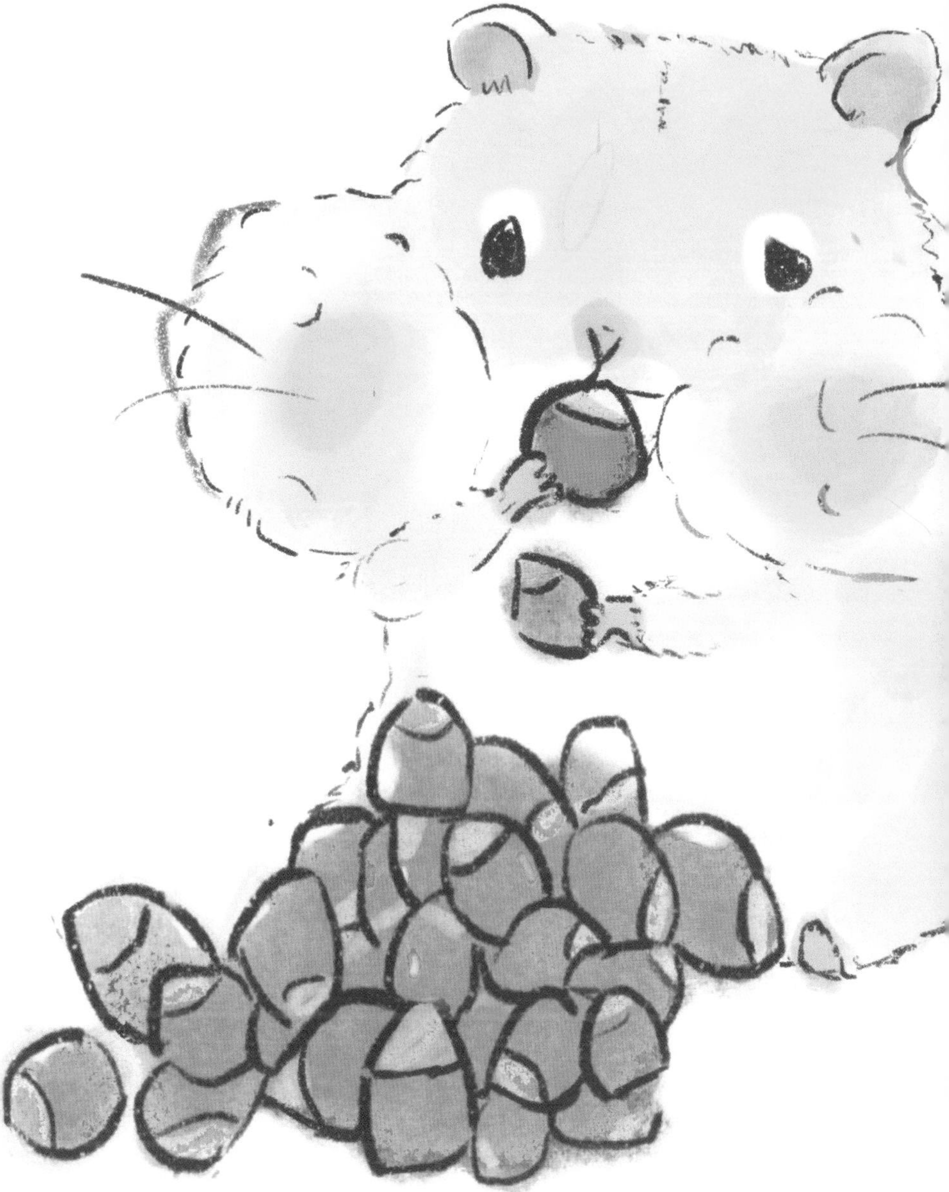

Chapter 7

Dr Dickson's Office

I saw mum talking to Dr Dickson in the corridor. He said something about me getting the two deaths mixed up. Mum's hair was a bit messy, she looked like she had just fallen out of bed and come to school.

Dr Dickson asked me lots of questions and then he said, 'Monica Pink you're in denial,' and I said, 'What does in denial mean?' And he said, 'Acting like you don't care.' So I pretended not to care by picking up a Personality Test from his desk.

A Personality Test has lots of questions and you answer them and then the test tells you what you are like. I read the questions and then Dr Dickson said lots of words that I didn't really understand but it was something like this, 'There are several stages of grief that everyone goes through, they are; Denial, Anger, Sadness and Acceptance. But one day you will learn to love again.'

I don't think he was talking to me any more - he was staring at mum. Mum then said, 'Monica would like a new pet.'

And then Dr Dickson said he thought getting a new pet was a very good idea and then I didn't know what to think about Dr Dickson anymore because more than anything I'd like a new pet.

Dr Dickson said he was allergic to pets himself - so I threw Henry the Hamster at him.

We nearly escaped but then Dr Dickson gave mum some Pink Perky Pills and told her they would make her feel a whole lot better. He then said, **'I'd really like to see Monica in her home environment,'** and then he invited himself to dinner.

'Why don't I pop round and make you both dinner, say Saturday around 7pm?' Mum just nodded a yes. I think Dr Dickson is far too clever for me.

I went back to class and Mark Dickson stopped me at the door and said, 'Been to see the Shrink, Psycho Pink?' And then he said, 'Now, I'll know all your secrets.'

I wish Fearless Fred would bash Mark Dickson and his sneaky snake uncle.

Chapter 8

The Animal Sanctuary

I watched mum take some of her Pink Perky Pills, her eyes nearly popped out of her head.

I went over to William's house. William has lots and lots and lots of pets. They are all over the house and garden and outbuildings. I don't think I have ever seen so many pets or been so happy. I talked to Kevin the budgie and told him my name over and over and then he said, 'Hello.'

I love Kevin the budgie.

William told me some stuff about Budgies.

1. Budgies can live until they are 27.

2. Budgies like warm wind because they are from Australia.

3. If you teach your budgie to say your name and address then someone will always bring him home.

I wonder if budgies like to share their cages with other budgies. I know that lovebirds like to share their cages but I don't know if you get love budgies.

We went into the kitchen and I met

William's crazy haired dad. William's dad is called Joe Strange and I like him. He said to me, 'I like your outfit, Monica Pink.'

Joe Strange is the first person to have noticed that I was in black. I said, 'My tortoise died,' and Joe Strange said, 'I'm very sorry for your loss.'

Joe Strange is funny and he loves all pets and all animals and he really likes talking. He was washing a duck in the sink but he could still answer the questions from my Personality Test. I asked him five questions and then he asked me what his personality was and I said he was normal and he said, 'Glad to hear it, Monica Pink.'

Five Personality Questions

Do you like inside or outside?
It depends on the time of year.

Do you like mornings or evenings?
Mornings.

Do you like vegetables or meat?
I like them both.

Do you like to be on your own or with
lots of people?
I like being with lots of pets, does
that count?

Do you hide when you are nervous?
No, I change the subject.

Joe Strange asked me how I knew so much about personality tests and I told him I had a shrink and he said I was really lucky and he wished he had a shrink and he wished all of his pets had a shrink. I asked him why his pets needed a shrink and he said; 'Monica, pets are just like us and sometimes they need a little help to get through the sad times.'

And then I had a brilliant idea and I said, 'Mr Strange, maybe I could be their shrink. I could be Monica Pink Pet Shrink,' and we all smiled and I think that it was the happiest second of my life.

And then Joe Strange farted and William said, 'A fart is the equivalent to my dad having a light bulb come on above his head. Farting means he's had an idea.'

Joe Strange laughed and said I could go and ask mum if she wanted to come over to dinner.

I asked him if I could have a goldfish to take home to cheer her up and he gave me Bob.

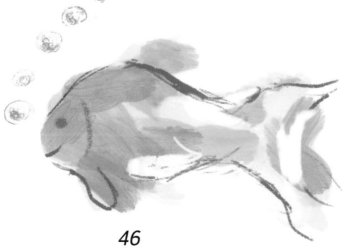

46

Chapter 9

Dinner at the Strange's

Mum looked different and her eyes seemed strange. Mum was angry with me and Bob. 'You cannot take pets from complete strangers!'

I tried to explain. 'He isn't a stranger, he is just called Mr Strange and it isn't a pet it's a fish and Mr Strange said we could eat him if we wanted.' Mum looked even angrier and said, 'I'm going to give Mr Strange a piece of my mind.'

I ran after her.

Mum rang the doorbell and Joe and William Strange answered. Joe Strange talked and talked and mum didn't say anything, she just stared at him and William with big, wide-open eyes. Joe Strange said how sorry he was that dad had died. He told us that when William's mum passed away William wore the same clothes for a year because he just wanted everything to be the same as it had been before his mum died. He said he knew what we were going through and then he asked if we liked Duck a l'Orange because that was what was for dinner. We sat down for dinner and mum still hadn't said anything.

Dinner was delicious, much better than mum's dinners and then Joe Strange asked us how we liked Horatio and mum spat her food out and me and William laughed. Mum ran out of the room to be sick.

Joe Strange has such a sweet face that I think people just want to tell him everything about themselves. He is like a big shaggy dog with his crazy hair, his big soft eyes and his giant smile. He is a big shaggy dog who can cook, look after pets and give out jobs.

Joe asked mum if she'd like to be pet groomer and work for him in the animal sanctuary and mum said, 'Not on your life Mr Strange.'

As mum dragged me off, I asked mum if I could be a Pet Shrink and mum said, 'What do you know about pets?'

I asked Joe Strange if I could have Kevin the budgie to take home with me so that I could practice being a Pet Shrink. Joe Strange told me that Kevin the budgie was a little bit sad because he missed his mum and I promised that I would do my best to cheer him up.

I tried to teach Kevin to say, 'There's no air in here,' just in case someone decided he should work down a mine.

I let Kevin the budgie sleep in my room in case he was lonely on his first night in a new house. Kevin was kind of noisy, he kept pecking the bars of his cage.

I went through to tell mum that I couldn't sleep but she was snoring really loudly. Her Pink Perky Pills were at the side of the bed. I looked at the leaflet inside the box. I wrote down what it said:

Risk of palpitations, skin rash or hives; difficulty breathing; swelling of your face, lips, tongue, or throat. Call your doctor at once if you have any new or worsening symptoms such as: mood or behavior changes, anxiety, panic attacks, trouble sleeping, or if you feel impulsive, irritable, agitated, hostile, aggressive, restless, hyperactive (mentally or physically), more depressed, or have thoughts about hurting yourself...

Chapter 10

First Day At Work...

Today I am wearing pink socks and I have a pink ribbon in my hair. I still have a black armband on, I have written Speedy's name on the armband. Joe Strange said, 'My, you're looking in the pink.'

I don't really know what looking in the pink means – but it sounds nice.

Me and William sat in my Pet Shrink office and waited for our first pet. William is going to be my note-taking assistant because he likes writing lots of facts in his notebook. We waited for ages and ages but nobody knocked on the Pet Shrink door. William pulled my hair and we played a game of chasing. I chased him all the way into the Pet Grooming Salon.

Jessica Parker, the goody-two-shoes, swotty girl from school, knocked on the door of the salon. She said her poodle was called Olivia Wainright the Third and that she answers to Pinky. William stood next to Jessica and told her lots of facts about

poodles, but Jessica didn't look interested.

William's Poodle Facts

1. Poodles are very popular in France and in 1500 they made them their national dog.
2. Poodles are also very good at hunting, especially in water.
3. Poodle is a German word for puddle.

I took Olivia Wainright the Third to the washbasin for a shampoo and set. I accidentally used green gooey hand cleaner instead of shampoo and Olivia

Wainright the Third turned a funny shade of green. When Jessica saw her poodle, she screamed and ran out of the salon.

Olivia Wainright the Third is the first ever pet to come to my Pet Shrink office.

Olivia sat up on the couch and I sat in a chair and took notes. I told Olivia that she had to accept herself as she was but she didn't look very interested and so I said, 'You're in denial Olivia.'

Olivia looked straight into my eyes and I said, 'I know what it is like to be abandoned by the person who is meant to be looking after you.'

Olivia looked very sad and I had to wipe away my tears and then wipe her eyes.

Today I also found out that Olivia Wainright the Third is really good at keeping secrets, I told her about Fearless Fred, The Lion Tamer and she looked happy that my dad was still alive and hiding in the circus.

I looked out of the window and there was a queue of kids from school outside the hut with their pets. I smiled and Olivia wagged her tail.

Chapter 11

More Funerals

Dr Sneaky Snake Dickson came for dinner. He cooked a very big fish on the big cooker in the kitch-en. The fish stared at me with its black eyes and it looked alive. I asked mum how the fish died and Dr Dickson said maybe the fish had caught a cold or something, I looked over at Bob in his fish bowl and worried that he might catch cold too.

I asked Dr Dickson if Speedy had gone to Pet Heaven and before he could answer mum said that Dr Dickson had brought us chocolates and then Dr Dickson said chocolate sends happiness endorphins to the brain.

And then I had an idea.

During the night, I snuck into the kitchen and put Bob's bowl on the cooker so that he wouldn't catch cold overnight and then I pushed some chocolate through Kevin's bars to cheer him up. Kevin tweeted with happiness as the chocolate hit his head.

I woke up this morning to hear my mum screaming. I ran through to the living room and Kevin was hanging upside down on his perch and his face was covered in chocolate. Dr Dickson was there too and I said he told me that chocolate made you happy and he said, 'I didn't say stuff your budgie's face in it.'

Mum screamed again. Bob the fish was lying at the bottom of an empty bowl. Mum said his water had boiled dry because the range cooker is on all the time.

I buried Bob and Kevin next to Speedy. Joe and William came to the funeral, they wore white. Mum let me wear a black veil over my head. Mum had set the garden up for an after funeral garden party. There was a table covered with drinks and

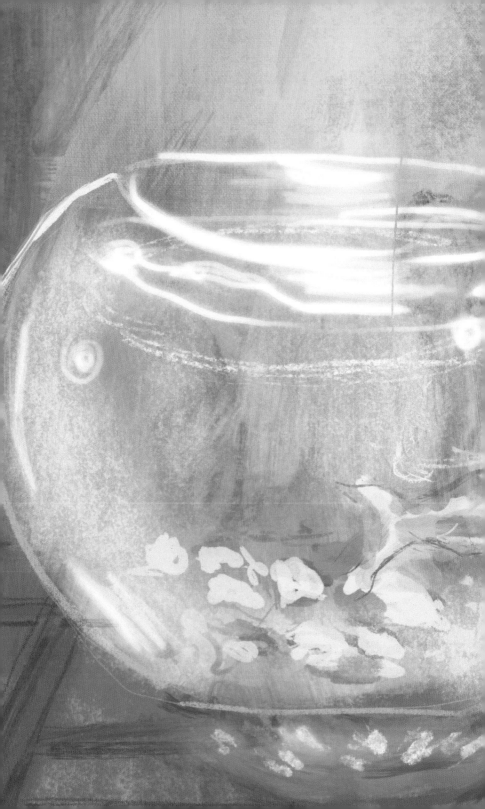

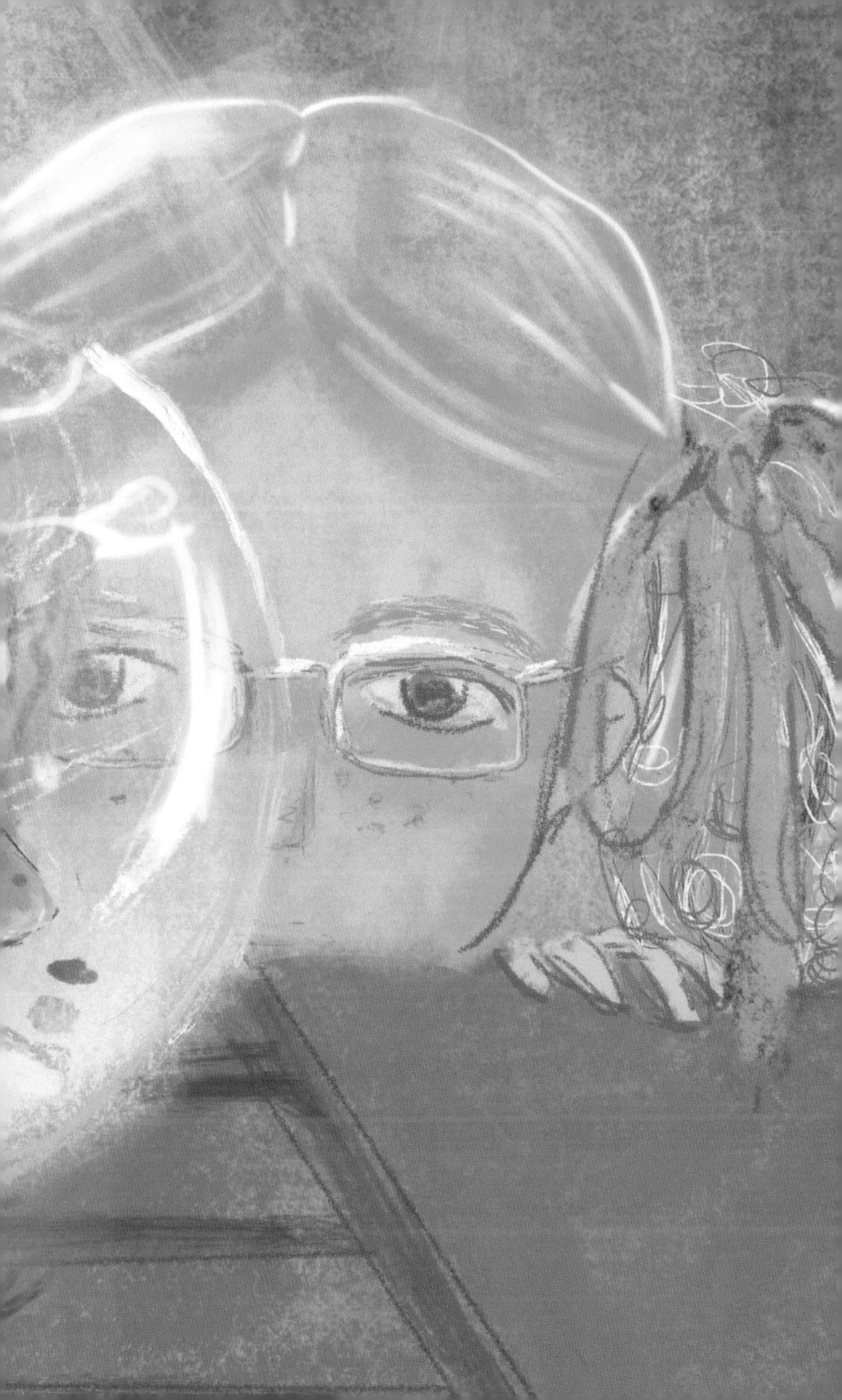

snacks. Dr Dickson, Miss Appleby and some kids from school (along with their pets) had come. Jessica was there with her green Poodle and even nasty Mark was there with his mangy old dog, Fido. Dr Dickson kept sneezing when he was near Fido.

Dr Dickson said it was my fault that Bob died. He said, '**I didn't tell you to boil the thing alive.**'

Mum had to take a side and she took mine. Dr Dickson was so angry he tripped up over Fido and nearly broke his neck - all the kids from school gasped.

Chapter 12

Enlist Support

The kids followed me to the pet shrink office. I told them that Dr Dickson was a pet killer and that he won't stop until every pet in the village has died mysteriously. And then Mark burst in and said, 'Monica Pink is a pet killer, she was alone when her pets died.'

I was so angry I threw my toy tortoise at him. The kids gasped again and covered their pets.

'You're in denial Monica Pink Psycho Shrink.'

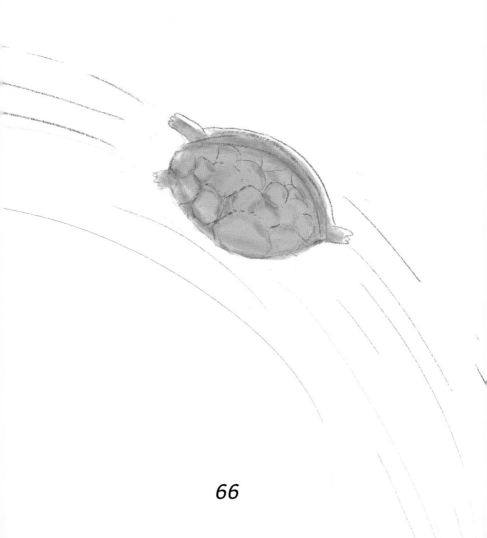

Chapter 13

Get Grown Up Help

I looked up all of the numbers I could find for circuses and I called them all. I left a message - it went like this.

'Hello Fearless Fred, please come home. Dr Dickson is a pet killer and he is trying to steal mum.'

I then decided I had to tell mum. She was sitting on the floor, she was surrounded by chocolate wrappers and her Pink Perky Pills were next to her. I just blurted out, 'Mum dad isn't really dead he has just gone to the circus.' Mum looked confused for a second and then she said, 'He never let me eat chocolate and now that he's gone to his circus in the sky, I can do what I want. I could eat chocolate forever.'

I was so angry with mum for not listening to me that I threw the chocolates box into the bin but it was empty so it just sort of floated in.

The next day I went to speak to Mr Strange but he was busy with the animals and he said, 'Sometimes things just happen and it's really nobody's fault.'

Well that's just wrong because it's Dr Dickson's fault.

Chapter 14

Gather Evidence

As no grown-ups were going to help I decided to gather the evidence to prove to them that Dr Dickson is a pet killer. I made William help me. We went around the village and took photos of all of the pet graves in kids' gardens. I had to give William my infra-red see-in-the-dark spectacles to make him come with me.

William put up a big map of the village in the pet shrink hut and we put up all the pictures of the graves and a photo of Dr

Dickson's car. We drew lines between all of the graves. A light-bulb went off in my head but I didn't fart. I said, 'He's a serial killer.' And then William farted and he said, 'Maybe he cut the brakes of the lawn mower to kill Speedy and your dad so that he could marry your mum.'

And then I told William, 'My dad has actually run away to the circus and he's Fearless Fred the lion tamer.'

William answered, 'That doesn't mean that Dr Dickson didn't try to kill him.' I grabbed William's hand - he thought we were going to the circus but we went to the police station. We sat in front of Inspector Charlie McGowan. I told him the story and he laughed until he nearly fell off his chair.

Next we went to the lawnmower outhouse in the garden. William thought we needed fingerprint evidence. He tipped a bag of white cement over the tractor and the dust went all over my specs. I lost my temper and shouted, '**Maybe killing him would be easier.**'

William took me seriously and wrote down a list under the heading, **Ways to Kill Dr Death**. We came up with some plans from films, like chucking him over a waterfall in a barrel, blowing him up in a train going over a bridge. I told William we were just a couple of kids and we would never be able to get rid of Dr Dickson.

William said we should poison him with poison frog goo.

We heard our names being shouted by Mr Strange, we ran outside and found Mr Strange on the trampoline with a new puppy. William called the puppy Monica.

Chapter 15

Good Grief

Today at school we had to draw pictures of our lost, disappeared and dead pets. I drew a picture of Speedy. Mark Dickson drew a picture of a grave and wrote **Monica the puppy RIP**. William was really angry he pulled Mark Dickson's hair and tried to punch him. He shouted, '**You want to kill my dog, you're a pet killer just like your uncle, Dr Death.**'

Miss Appleby was really upset and she sent us to Dr Dickson's office. Dr Dickson said, '**Dr Death now that's not very nice, is** it children?'

We had to say sorry, luckily I had my fingers crossed behind my back. Dr Dickson made Mark stay behind.

We climbed on a table and looked though the window. Dr Dickson hit Mark. Mark is mean but his uncle is even meaner. Mark is caught up in a bicycle of meanness and the only way for him to change is to get away from his Uncle Dr Death.

William really annoyed me today, he keeps asking when we are going to the circus. He said I was a scaredy-cat so I slammed the school classroom door in his face.

Chapter 16

Poison Goo

Today we tried to cover Dr Dickson in poison frog goo. William was hiding in the rafters and I was on the school stage, we were practicing for the school show. I managed to stop Dr Dickson by asking him about his book, Explaining Pet Deaths to Children. All William had to do was drop the goo, he did drop it but at the wrong time and it went all over me. Poison frog goo doesn't turn kids into frogs, only nasty grown-ups. I did burp like a frog a couple of times.

When I got home Dr Dickson's bags were in the hall. HE'S MOVING IN. Now Dad will never come home and it's all my fault 'cause I let Speedy poo on the floor and I didn't manage to get rid of Dr Dickson.

Mum shouted at me because I was covered in goo and because I shouted at Dr Dickson, 'Are you going to hit me the way you hit Mark?'

And Dr Dickson said, 'Leave her Barb, anger is a perfectly normal stage for her to be going through.'

I was going to slam the door but I didn't want him to see I was angry. I heard him say, 'Sometimes I think, I would make a great step-dad. Marry me Barb, I'm crazy about you.'

I was now so angry I smashed up my Pet Shrink office. A little piglet watched me and I even shouted at him too.

Chapter 17

House-trained

I went to find William but he wasn't talking to me, he bounced on the trampoline as if I wasn't there. I told him he was being silly and he said he wasn't the one who believed their dead dad was a lion tamer. And I said, 'Nobody wants to marry your dad cause he isn't even house-trained.'

Mum had said that once. Unluckily for me Mr Strange was standing behind me and he looked really sad.

I found dad's bow and arrows in the

chest in the attic. I aimed it at Dr Dickson's head as he was going through papers in dad's office. He dropped the papers and jumped up and down singing, 'She's worth a fortune.'

He was jumping up and down so much I couldn't get a clear aim and then he skipped out of the room singing, 'Soon I'll be rich, rich, rich.'

I looked at the paper he was looking at and it said, The last will and testament of Ken Pink.

I ran over to tell William, but he wouldn't listen and wouldn't take his earphones out.

I ran into the house but Mr Strange was hoovering and he couldn't hear me.

Dr Dickson was pretending to be a great gardener and was working in the garden. I hid in the rafters with a catapult and waited. Dr Dickson came in for the pitchfork. He bent down and picked up William's notebook with the notes: **Ways to Kill Dr Death.** He threw the pitchfork into the ground, it went right through my toy rabbit - he stormed out and I fell out of the rafters.

I'm not allowed to play at William's house anymore and I'm not allowed to go to my

Pet Shrink office. Dr Dickson said, 'You don't have any clients and none of the kids like you - so what's the problem?'

But just when I thought things couldn't get any worse I heard Dr Dickson telling mum that I should go to a boarding school for disturbed children. He then said, 'I will see to it that they get her medication just right.'

He's going to put me on Baby Perky Pills and then I will be as mad as mum.

I now have no choice, I have to run away to the circus.

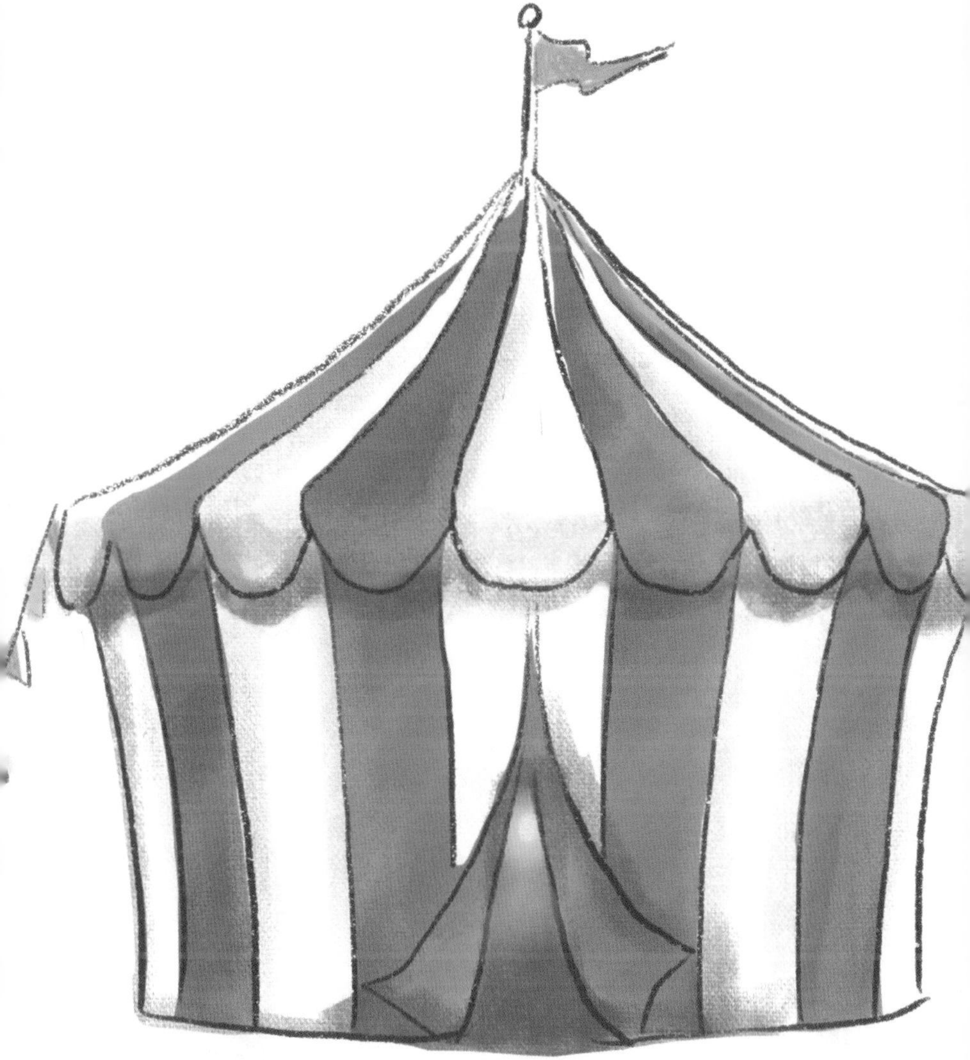

Chapter 18

First Escape

I packed my rucksack with a jar of Nuttela and Fearless Fred's lion taming whip. I emptied mum's Pink Perky Pills in the toilet and replaced them with sweeties. I put in my toy rabbit for luck - even though the rabbit wasn't very lucky and got jabbed with a pitchfork. I took my torch and said goodbye to the animals in the sanctuary. I saw Williams lights go on and I made a run for it.

I ran across a big field and reached the

forest, it was dark and scary in the woods and so I ran very fast. I lost my Wellington boot but kept running. I got to the end of the wood and saw a stable on the hill, I ran to the stable cause I knew the horses would look after me.

Interesting facts about horses:

1. If you want to know how old a horse is you just have to count his teeth.
2. A foal's legs are too long for the foal to be able to reach down and eat grass - so their mums have to feed them.

3. Horses use their tails to send
   messages to one another about how
   they are feeling.

I lay down next to a foal and the foal sniffed my hair, that's a foal's way of saying hello. I felt safe and warm and feel asleep. I woke up because something kicked me. I looked up and William was standing there wearing my infra-red specs. He was holding my Wellington boot and had Monica the puppy on a lead. He said, 'Didn't get very far without me,' and I said, 'That's 'cause you weren't helping me.'

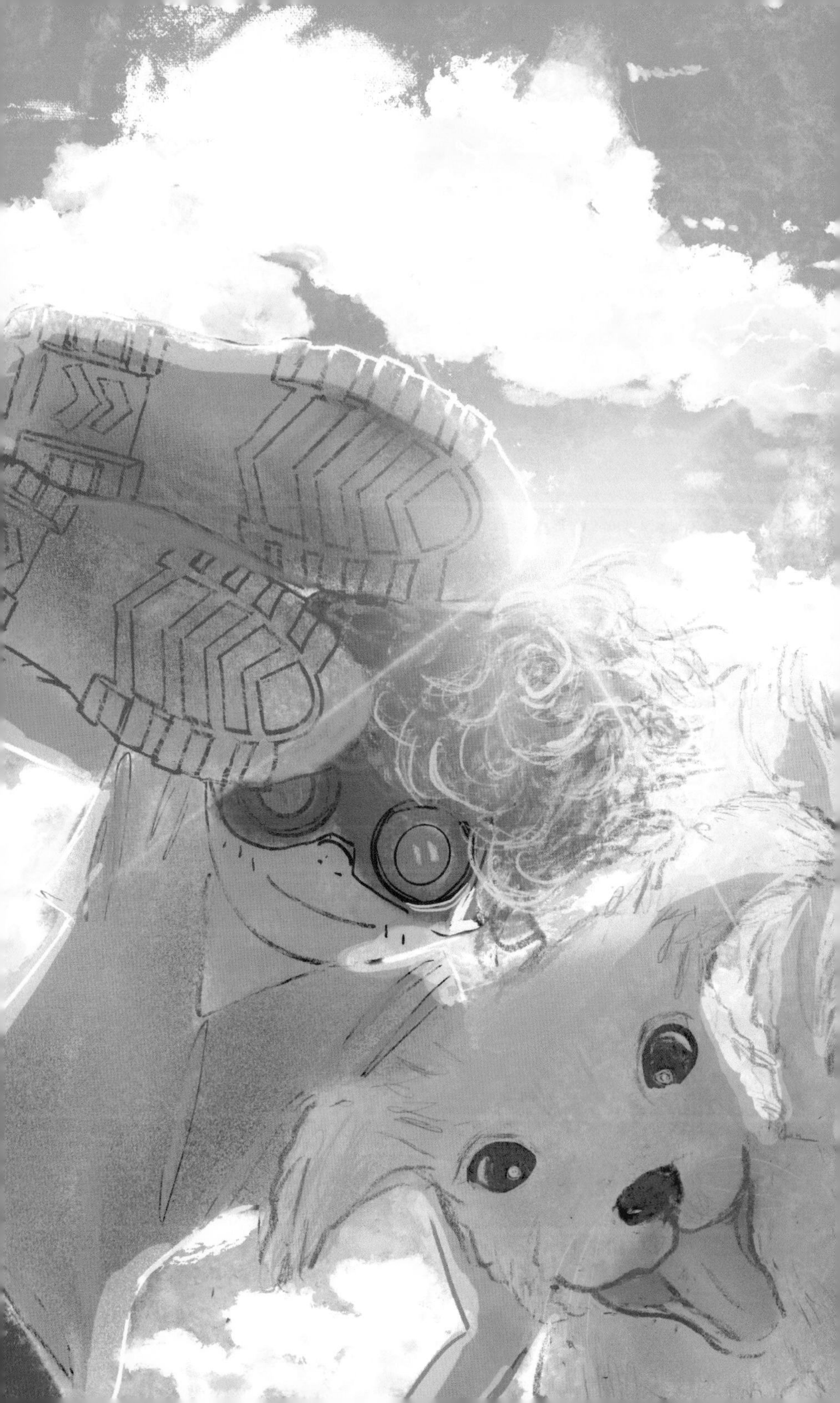

Chapter 19

Second Escape

We decided that William would work the brakes and I would work the steering. Dr Dickson's car is small enough for a couple of kids to drive. I put Monica the puppy in her travel box and sat her on the passenger seat. Monica looked happy to be part of our adventure, she doesn't like being left out.

I don't really want to talk about driving on the big road - I was really scared but I had to be brave for Monica the puppy and

William. A big truck drove very close to us all the way along the big road, I think they were trying to protect us. I saw a sign for The Hilltop Circus. I shouted to William to brake and I turned the car to the pavement.

We banged into the pavement and I flew out of the front of the car onto the bonnet. William banged his head, Monica the puppy got a fright but she was alright.

We ran all the way to the top of the hill. This tiny baby circus was just waking up. We went into a tent where a teenager all dressed in black was juggling on a unicycle.

She was really good but she looked like she didn't even care that she could juggle and cycle.

William went straight up to her and asked if we could get a shot on the unicycles - she shrugged her shoulders. I asked if I could let the doves out and again she shrugged her shoulders.

I asked the teenager where the lions were and she said we were in the wrong circus. I told her my dad was Fearless Fred and she laughed so much she fell off her unicycle. William told her that we were runaways and then we had to run as she was going to tell on us.

We ran away on the unicycles. She shouted after us, 'Life's a game and we all die in the end.'

I think teenagers are weird.

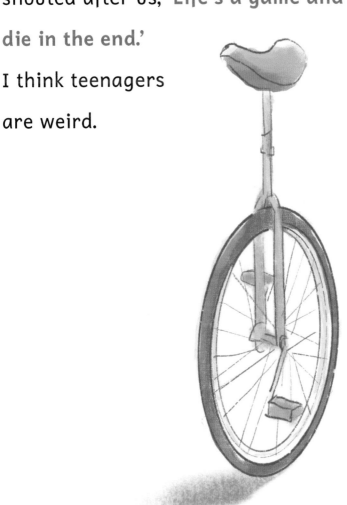

Chapter 20

The Real
Fearless Fred

We had to get off the unicycles and push them because the hills were difficult and Monica the puppy couldn't keep up. There were lots of things going on in the streets. It was amazing, there were men breathing fire, girls on stilts and performing Poodles. Poodles are show-offs so I don't think they minded having to be performers.

Monica the puppy ran over to say hello to a dog on a rope that was sitting beside a teenager who was a bit smelly. I asked the teenager if he would take us to the circus. And he said, 'Why?'

So I told him that I was a Pet Shrink. I thought that it would be a good idea if his dog had a walk, and he got up and led the way.

As we were following him, William suddenly grabbed my arm and pointed into a shop that had TVs on. We saw pictures of ourselves and then mum and Joe Strange and Dr Dickson talking. Dr Dickson pushed a copy of his book in front of the camera and mum looked really angry. I put the hood up on my hoodie and we ran to catch up with the smelly teenager and his dog.

We turned a corner and there in front of us was the greenest grass and the biggest red and white circus tent ever. The smelly teenager's dog jumped for joy and so did Monica the puppy.

William said, 'I wish it was as easy to find my mum.' And I said, 'But your mum isn't hiding, she's dead.'

And William said, 'Yes but if she wasn't dead and she was hiding I wish it was easy. I wish she was on TV and worked in a circus.'

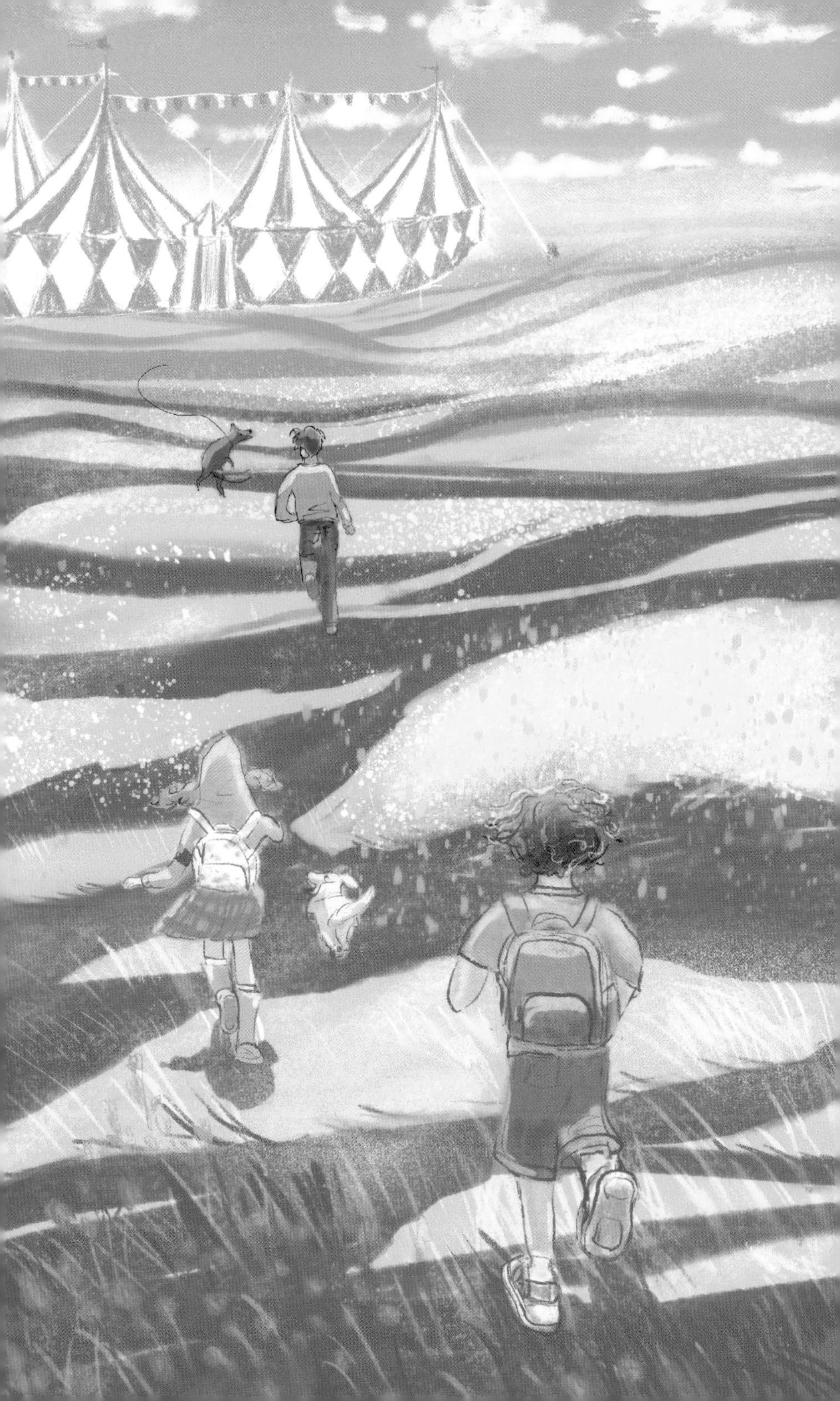

I suppose I am lucky.

Me and William ran towards the tent. Everything was all closed up but we snuck behind where all the trucks and cages were. I stared in at the elephants. Most of them looked pretty bored. I asked William what they were thinking and he said, 'They're thinking, I hope my teeth don't fall out.'

I stopped at the white horses and William wandered off to look at the circus dogs. I found the Nutella in my bag and put some on my hand, I held my hand out and the horsey licked it. I told the horsey that chocolate sends happiness dolphins to the brain and then I heard a lion roar.

I took my lion tamer's whip out of my bag and went over to the lion's cage. I opened the padlock with my clasp and I climbed into the cage. I stared straight into the lion's eyes and I felt a message of love go between us. The lion's whiskers moved and he sat up on his paws ready to pounce, luckily I had my lion tamer's whip behind my back. I held onto it really tightly. I was just about to swing the whip when I was pulled out of the cage.

I screamed and the old man dressed

like Fearless Fred screamed. He shouted words at me in a funny language. I didn't understand so he shouted in a funny voice.

'What the hell do you think you're doing?'

'Why are you wearing my dad's clothes?' I shouted back.

'Where did you get my lion-taming whip?' William arrived and shouted really loudly, 'Who are you?' We all calmed down at once.

The old man in my dad's lion taming outfit said, 'I'm Fearless Fred.'

And then I got really upset and I cried.

The old man looked upset too when I told him that Fearless Fred was my dad. He took us to a café for breakfast and he said he would do his best to explain everything.

We sat on red seats, the TV was on, me and William could see the TV but the old man couldn't. The waitress brought us all hot chocolate and toast. The old man said he was Fearless Fred and the programmes I watched were old re-runs of his show.

He said he once had a wife and a son called Kenneth. He said that his wife had run away and changed their name to Pink. He said my dad was his son and that he was my granddad and his eyes filled with tears. He told me I was half Russian and that my name was Monica Pinkovsky. I think I prefer Monica Pink.

The waitress had been listening and she said, 'He's your grandpa.' And I said, 'I don't have a grandpa.' And Fearless Fred smiled and said, 'You do now.' And William said 'Are you my grandpa too?' and Fearless Fred laughed.

I told Fearless Fred everything that had happened. I told him about Dr Dickson cutting the brakes of the lawnmower to kill dad and Speedy and marry mum. About

Dr Dickson killing my pets, the Pink Perky Pills and how he was going to send me to boarding school.

Fearless Fred scratched his head and said, 'Sounds like a bad'un to me.' He then asked us to stay for the matinee show - he said he would come up with a plan after the show. Just as he was going I said, 'Is my dad really dead?' He couldn't answer because he was crying but he gave me a big hug.

Me and William stared at the TV. Mum and Mr Strange were on again, We couldn't hear what they were saying but mum looked like she had been crying. Dr Dickson was in the background, he looked bored. Mr Strange held up the armadillo and waved its paw... he mouthed, '**Please come home kids.**'

Luckily the waitress didn't see it 'cause if she had she would have told on us.

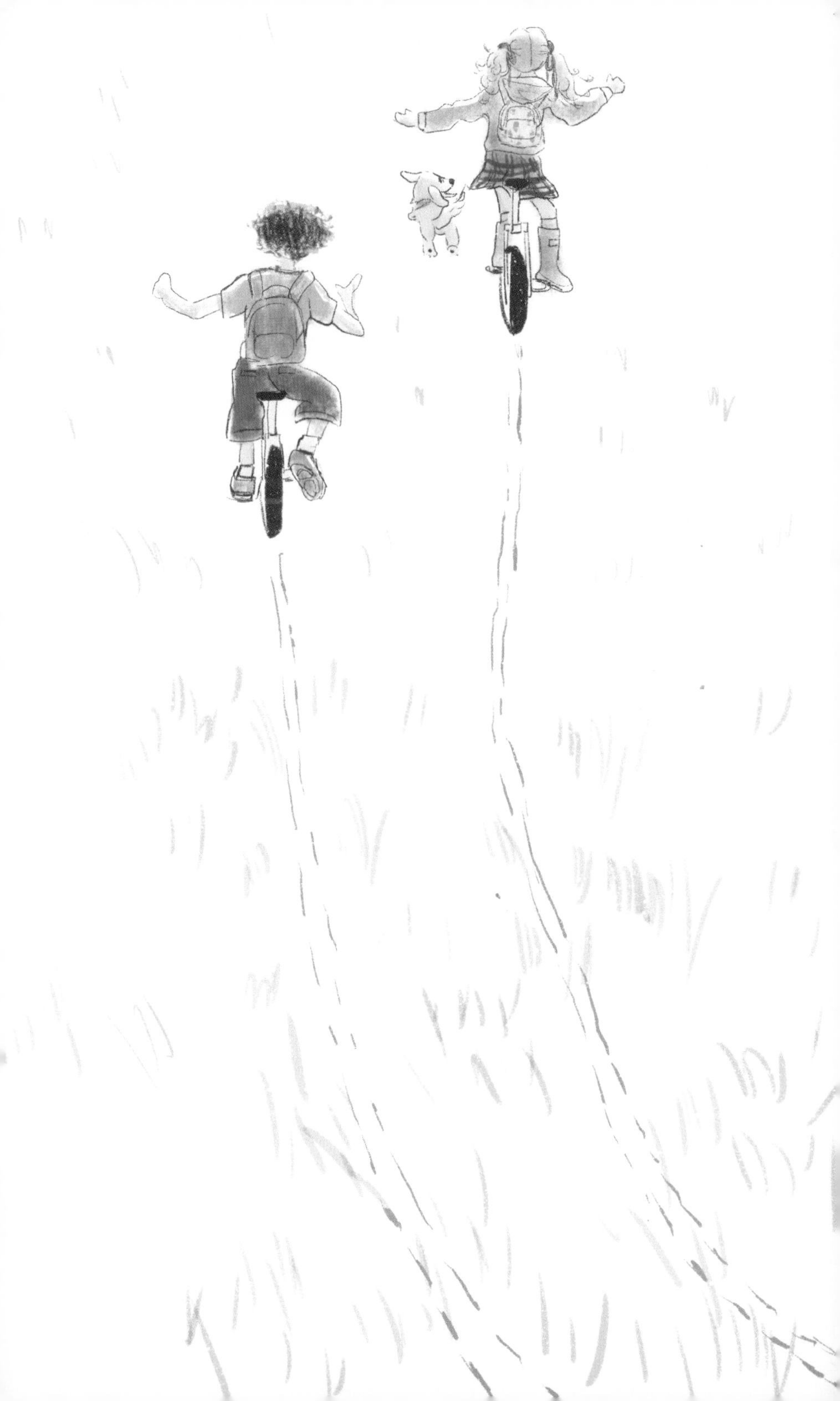

Chapter 21

The Circus

Me, William and Monica the puppy sat in the front row. We watched the ladies on white horses. One of the horses smiled at me. I think he was looking for more chocolate. Then there were the clowns, they fell over a lot and then we watched dogs jumping through hoops of fire. I asked William if he thought the fire-dogs could save people from burning buildings and he said, 'No.'

The lights went out, there was a drum roll and a voice said, 'And now ladies and gentlemen, boys and girls, our very own lion tamer, the one and only Fearless Fred.'

Everyone clapped and cheered and then Fearless Fred came into the circus ring and the spotlight came on.

I know he is my grandpa and everything but Fearless Fred was amazing. He spoke in a strange language to the lions and they did everything he said. William said that circus lions only understand Russian. He also said that circus lions don't have any teeth but I'm not sure if that's true.

At the end of the show the spotlight went onto me, William and the puppy –

Fearless Fred asked us to join him in the ring. We all hugged and William said to my grandpa, 'You smell of lions.'

I think William might be a little bit jealous that I have a grandpa - but I will ask Fearless Fred if it's okay if I share him.

We waited outside Fearless Fred's caravan and he came out all dressed in his Sunday clothes, but he hadn't combed his hair so he looked a bit strange. He shouted, 'I have a plan.' We clapped our hands with joy and then he said, 'I'll drive you home.'

Fearless Fred drove really slowly and lots of cars kept beeping their horns at us. His hair blew in the wind and he sang a sad little song to himself in lion taming language.

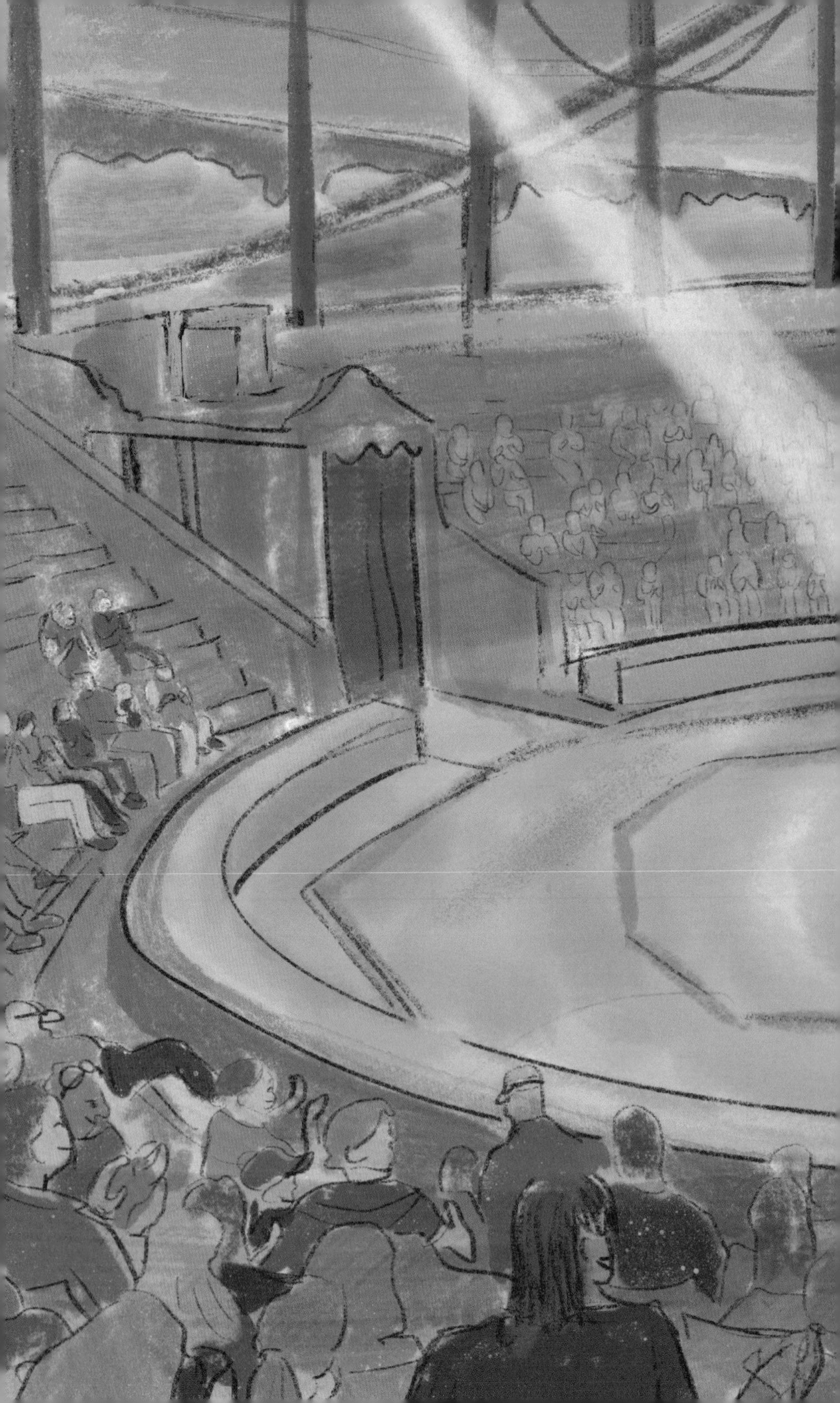

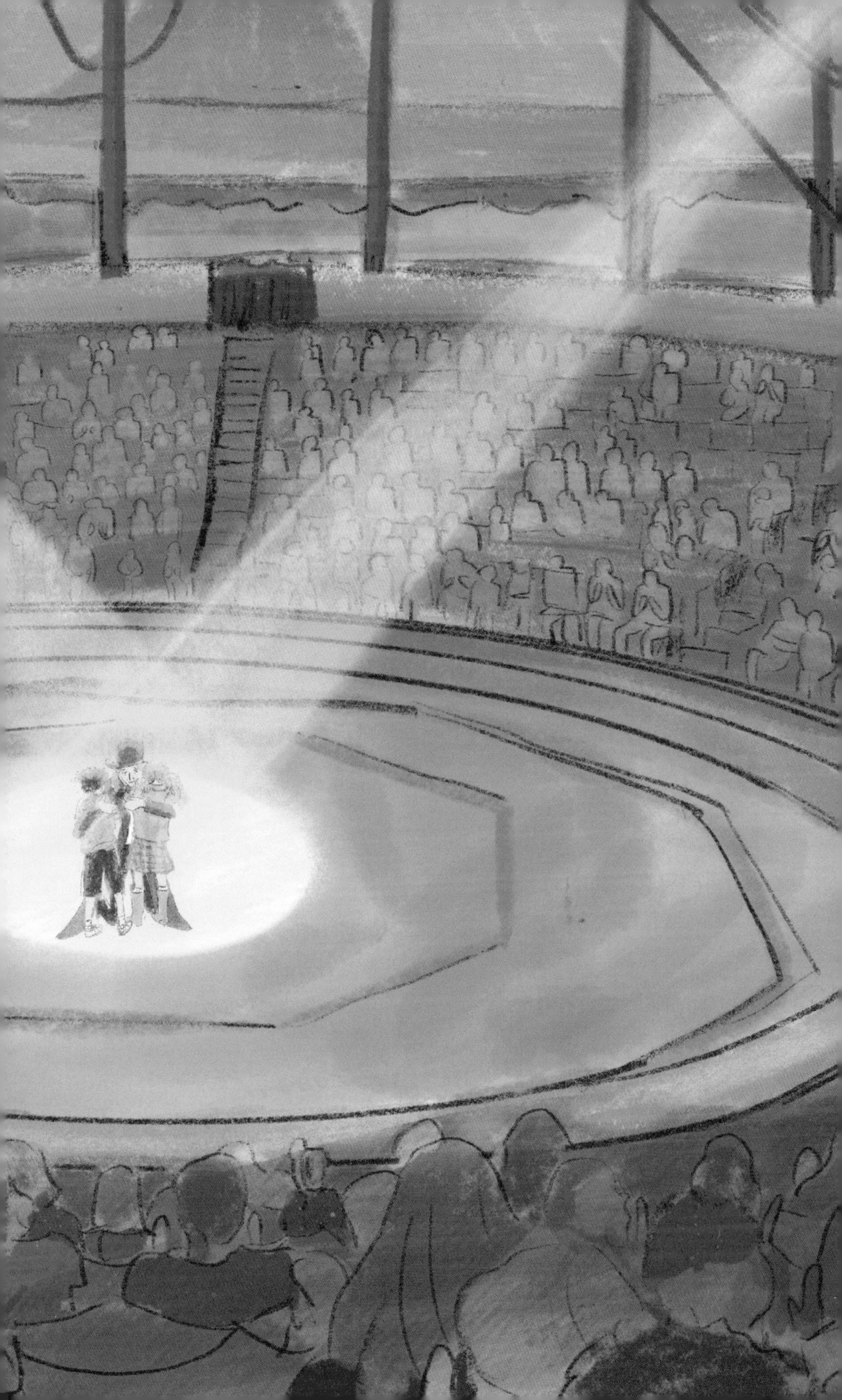

Chapter 22

Home Again

As we drove the crazy circus truck through my village, we heard police sirens and then we saw blue lights. Charlie, the police officer made us stop the truck. Fearless Fred turned to us and said, 'You kids wanted by the police?' And William said, 'We're runaways...' Fearless Fred sighed and said, 'Well if I'd known that...'

I don't think Fearless Fred is very good at being a grown up, I think he's just good at taming lions. William asked if Fearless Fred was going to prison and Fearless Fred said, 'I certainly hope not… I've got a show tonight.'

Then we all saw mum and Mr Strange running down the hill towards the truck. We all got out and I gave mum a big hug, she was very happy to see me. I explained everything that had happened and I told her that Fearless Fred was my grandpa. Mum said that dad had always said that he was from a Russian circus family but she had never believed him. She said, 'I thought he was just trying to make himself sound more interesting.'

Fearless Fred said something in Russian and mum looked amazed. Dad had lots of rules and he didn't let mum eat chocolate but I didn't know he was boring.

We all walked up to the house arm in arm but then a pick-up truck drove by with Dr Dickson's bashed up car on it. And I knew I was in trouble.

Dr Dickson came storming out of the house shouting, 'What have you idiot children done to my car?' William asked his dad if he was an idiot savant. Fearless Fred put up his fists, 'Stick 'em up,' he shouted, 'Who the hell are you?' said Dr Dickson. 'Only the father of the man you killed,' replied Fearless Fred. 'What man?' said Dr Dickson, trying to look innocent. So I shouted, 'You cut the brakes of my dad's lawnmower.'

Dr Dickson looked a little confused he said, 'This is ridiculous. Barb talk some sense into them.'

Mum didn't answer, she kept her arms folded. I don't think she likes Dr Dickson anymore.

I said, 'You're in denial Dr Dickson' and Mr Strange said, 'Are you even a proper shrink?'

Dr Dickson lost his temper and tried to push Fearless Fred out of the way. Fearless Fred landed a big fat punch on him - me and William cheered.

Mr Strange threw a ball and the puppy ran after it. Mr Strange told me and William to go and chase after the puppy before she got lost. So we had to go and we didn't get to see Dr Dickson crying.

Monica the puppy is a really fast runner and she was almost at the bridge before I caught up with her. William went off to look for the ball. Suddenly we heard a car screeching around the corner. It was Dr Dickson in his beat up car. He was going really fast and beeping his horn. The puppy stood still and so did I. Dr Dickson had to swerve really quickly to miss us both and his car flew off the bridge and into the river.

I said to the puppy, 'We killed him Monica pup, and now we will both have to go to jail.'

Charlie arrived in his police car and I put my hands up to be arrested. Then I heard Dr Dickson say, 'If the kid wants to take the blame then that's fine by me. Her mother's loaded. She can buy me a new car.'

William said, 'He didn't kill you or the puppy. Maybe we were wrong about him.' And I said, 'Maybe we were but he's still the meanest meaney ever.'

Chapter 23

Monica Pink Pet Shrink

There were a queue of kids waiting outside my office. Mr Strange said, 'Glad you could make it back to work Miss Pink.'

Mr Strange told me there were so many kids because Mark Dickson had told them that I was great and that Fearless Fred was my grandpa.

Mark Dickson was first in the queue with his sad looking dog, Fido, I told him that

Fido needed some self-steam, that you either have steam or you don't and that Fido had run out of steam. I told him to always be kind to Fido.

A kid with a tortoise came in next and I said, 'I'm sorry I don't treat tortoises.'

Me, mum and grandpa Fearless went to the graveyard. I took a picture of Speedy and stuck it to the grave and told dad I forgave him for killing Speedy and asked him to always look after him in heaven. Fearless Fred said to the gravestone, 'You have a lovely family son. I'm so proud of you.'

And I took grandpa Fearless' hand and said, 'We're proud of you too Grandpa.'

Fearless Fred put on a lion taming show with all the animals from the sanctuary. All the kids from school were there... it was the happiest day of my life.

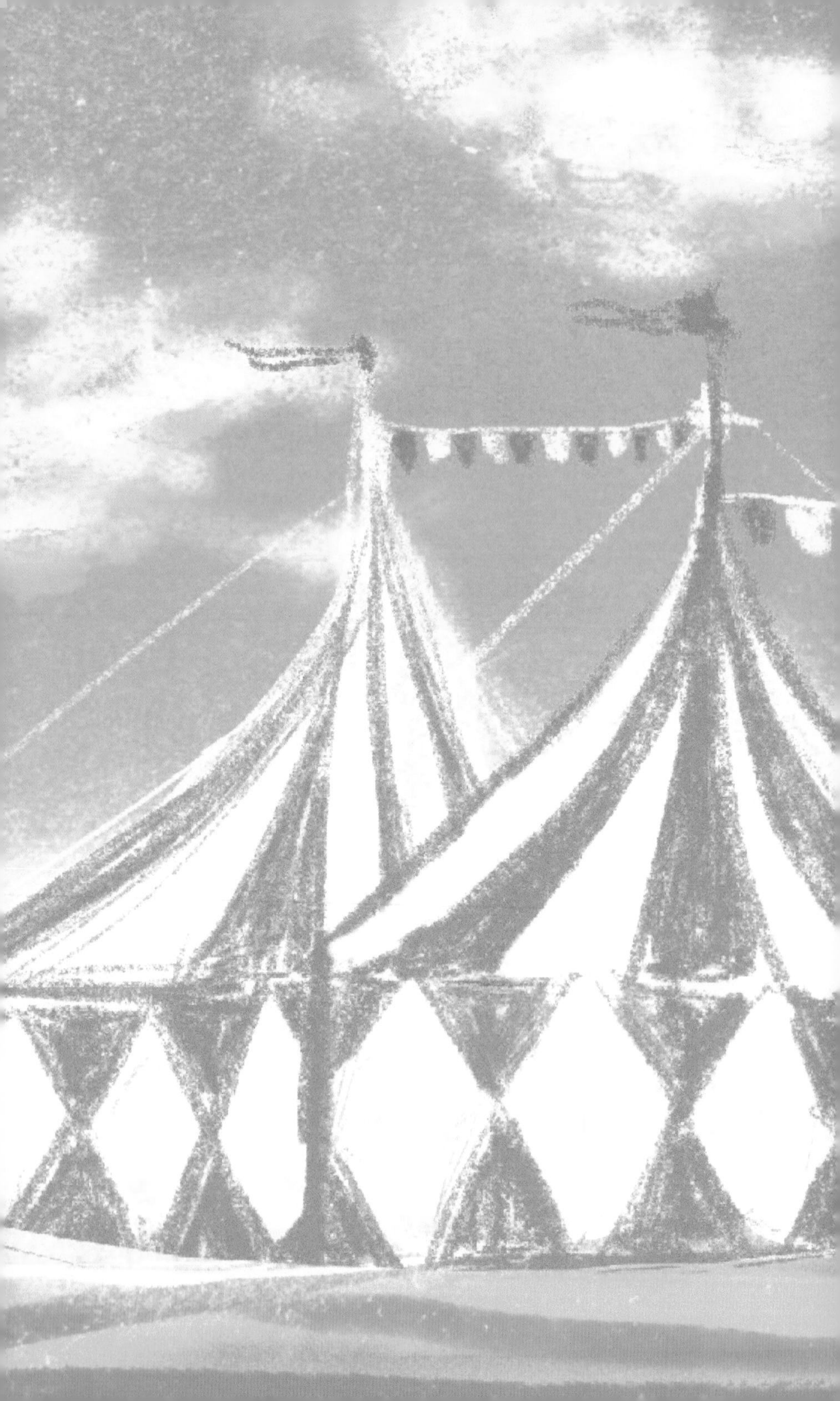

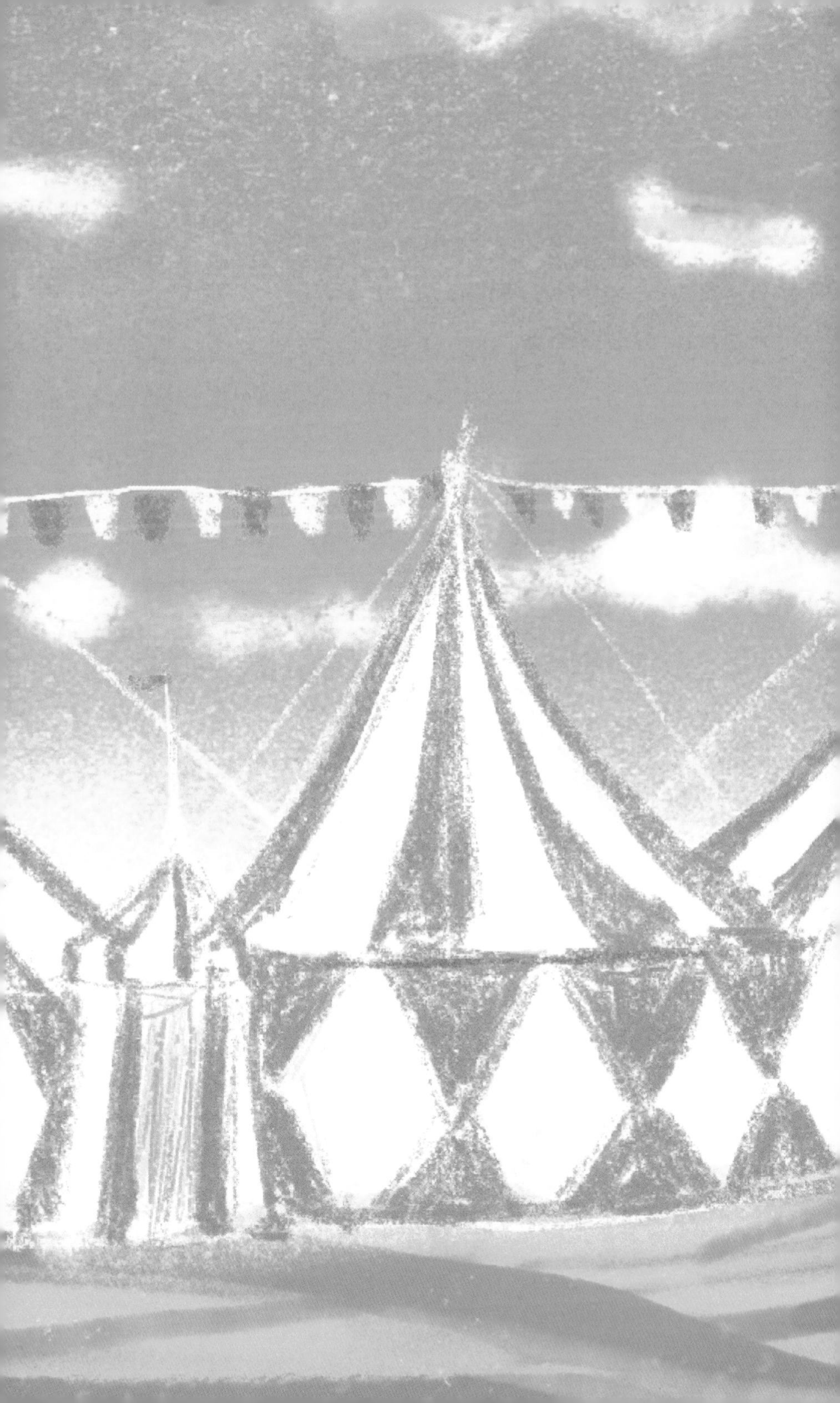

First published in 2021 by Sainted Media

Saintedmedia.com

ISBN: 9781916032934

eISBN: 9781838384937

Illustration: Xiaoyi Hu

Saintedmedia.com

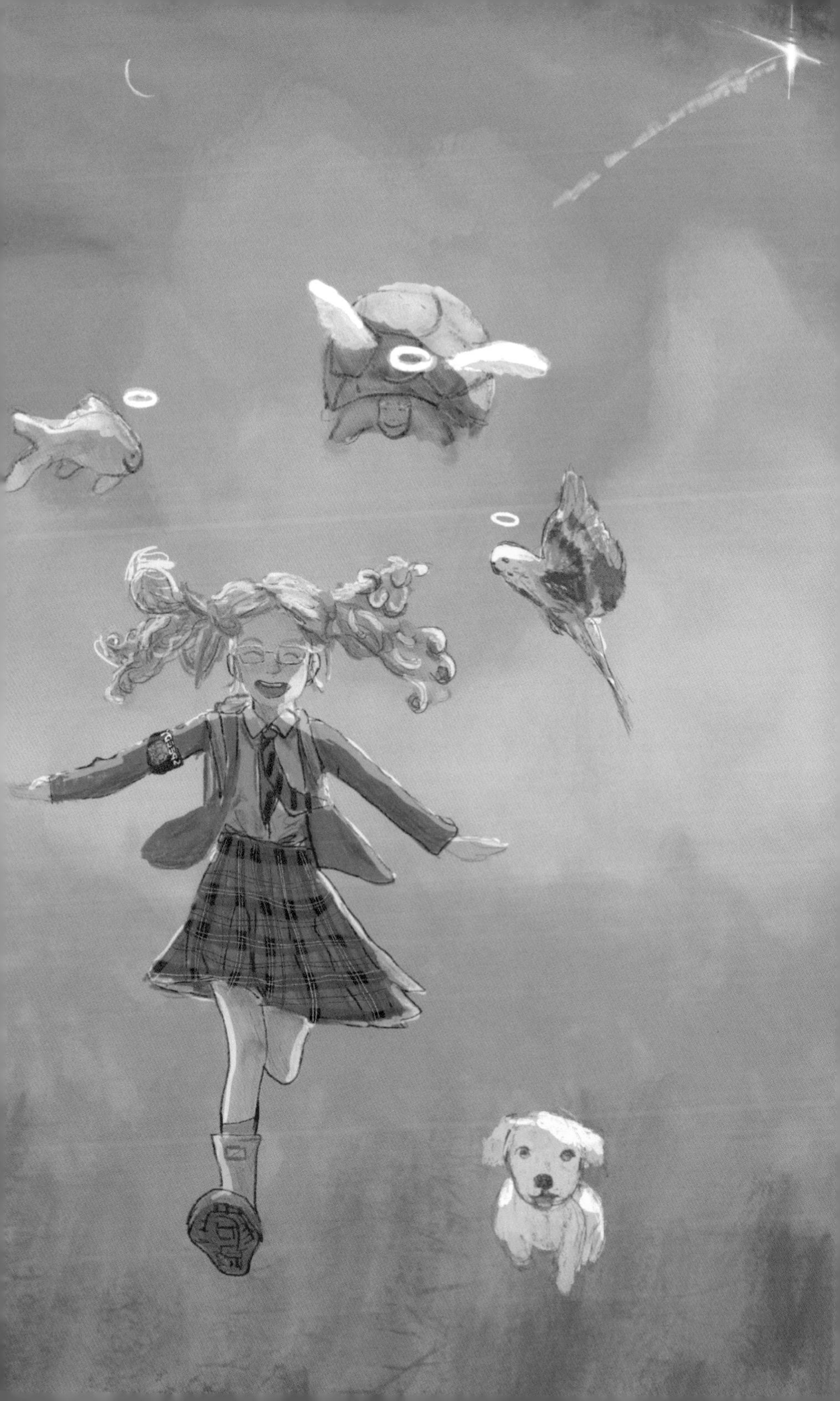

My Notes

. . . .

. . . .

. . . .

. . . .

. . . .

. . . .

. . . .

. . . .

. . . .

Printed in Great Britain
by Amazon